SELF-DISCOVERY

Let the one who has understanding calculate
the number of the beast

a book by

J.V.Q.A.

(Juan Vitaliano Quinonez Alban)

This is a book of self-discovery; you can experience the same I did or something completely different.

"SEEK AND YOU WILL FIND"

THIS PAGE INTENTIONALLY LEFT BLANK

ACKNOWLEDGMENT

This book is dedicated to all the German

speaking readers that bought my book:

Selbstentdeckung: Wer Verständnis hat, berechne die Zahl des Tieres

1. LET THE ONE WHO HAS UNDERSTANDING CALCULATE THE NUMBER OF THE BEAST

NOTE: This book was originally written in German

I never thought that so many Germans would be interested in many of my books. As a native Spanish speaker and also as an English translator, I apologize for any errors in this book as I do not speak German. But I wanted to share all the knowledge I have acquired since my youth to all my German readers.

The premise of this study is as follows:

"This calls for wisdom: let the one who has understanding calculate the number of the beast, for it is the number of a man, and his number is 666".

Apocalipsis 13:18 - English Standard Version

In order to fulfill the premise described above, the following steps must be done:

1. First, I need a scheme that sums to 666 using one or more sums.

$300 + 300 + 60 + 6 = 666$

$400 + 200 + 60 + 6 = 666$

$100 + 300 + 100 + 100 + 60 + 6 = 666$

We will select the scheme:

$$300 + 300 + 60 + 6 = 666$$

We need to find out in the Hebrew language which letters are in concordance with the scheme proposed $(300 + 300 + 60 + 6 = 666)$ according to Hebrew Gematria.

Shin = ש = 300

Samekh = ס = 60

Waw (vav) = ו = 6

$$ש \ (300) + ש \ (300) + o \ (60) + ı \ (6) = 666$$

שׁשׁ o ı

2. Then you may use your favourite translate website. In this case I use Google Translate (the translation is done from Hebrew to German because originally this book was aimed for German speakers)

We obtained "Psst" which would be the interjection of silence used in Germany.

3. Apparently, "Psst!" would be meaningless in terms of translation. However, some occultists use the interjection of silence as a warning that the subjects studied in the occult must be duly withheld or kept secret.

    I, J.V.Q.A., an Ecuadorian, South American author, am not an occultist, I am a Catholic, so I will speak or write whatever I find in this investigation.

All of the research we will see below is part of an apparent translation error. I call this method **IRRTUMLOGIE** (not to be confused with "Errorology").

If somehow I use an error to study anything related to divination, I would call it **IRRTUMANCIE**. However, since this is not the case, from now on everything that emerges from this research will fall under the realm of **IRRTUMLOGIE** (not to be confused with "Errorology" in English).

Please kindly read the definitions of **IRRTUMLOGIE** and **IRRTUMANCIE.**

Irrtumlogie. - (from Latin error: error, failure; and Greek logía: teaching) is a theoretical discipline that deals with paranormal, esoteric or eschatological phenomena from the perspective of error. **Irrtumlogie** is based on the assumption that human knowledge is always error-prone and insufficient, and that these errors can stimulate new ways of perceiving and interpreting reality. Irrtumlogie is not to be confused with irtumancie, a practical art of divination by error, nor with Errorology, an English term referring to the scientific study of errors and how to avoid them.

Irrtumancie. – (from Latin error: error, failure; and gr. mantéia: divination) is a practical art dealing with esoteric, paranormal and eschatological questions through the error. The **Irrtumancie** is based on the assumption that the error is a way of realizing hidden or future truths, and that these truths can be reached through rituals or means that provoke or take advantage of the error. **Irrtumancie** is not to be confused with Irrtumlogie, a theoretical discipline that examines errors as a source of knowledge.

4. Now let's rearrange the letters of the word שׁשׁסו and see what translation it gives us.

Before: שׁשׁסו = 666 (300+300+60+6)

After: שׁסוש =666 (300+60+6+300)

5. We may enter the word שׁסוש into Google Translate or another translator that allows translation from Hebrew to German.

שׁסוש = zögerte

Zögerte in English means "hesitated"

Zögerte. - Singular past tense indicative of hesitate (zögern in German). Hesitation means waiting indecisively before taking an action or decision, putting something off, not starting immediately or starting slowly. For example: He hesitated to pick up the phone. She hesitated to tell him the truth.

6. The words to find and the possible combinations are numerous, but based on my own experience we will focus on the following scheme: סשוש.

סשוש (60+300+6+300)

This word translated from Hebrew into German gives us the following translation:

DETECTAR IDIOMA   HEBREO   ALEMÁN   ESPAÑOL ⌄   ⇄   ALEMAN   ESPAÑOL   INGLES ⌄

סשוש ✕   Psst   ☆

Quizás quisiste decir: סשוש

🎤 ◀))   6 / 5.000   ◀))   ⬚ ⌂q ⋖

7. The next step is to find out which deity or god is associated with silence.

8. What is the name of the god of silence?

Vidar (Viðarr)

Vidar   Gott der **Stille**

In English: Vidar – God of Silence

The silent, vengeful and righteous Vidar the son of Odin and Gríðr in Norse mythology. He is one of the few gods alive after the end of the world who avenged his murdered father by defeating the giant wolf Fenrir. Vidar lives in a forest called Landvidi. He wears special shoes made of leather that people don't use. With these shoes, he can open Fenrir's mouth wide and tear his jaw.

9. We can use an artificial intelligence app or website to get better answers.

What is the name of the god or goddess of silence?

The artificial intelligence will answer something like: Harpocrates is the God of Silence. Harpocrates is the Greek name of the Egyptian god Horus, known as Horus the child. Harpocrates is associated with silence and secrecy.

In Roman mythology, the minor goddess Tacita, known as Tacita Muta, is associated with silence and secrecy by putting her finger to her lips or keeping her mouth closed. This gesture, also known as the Harpocrates gesture, is well known.

10. After that, we can consult our preferred web browser; in this case it would be Google. How does Harpocrates relate to the occult?

Harpocrates is a figure of special importance in occultism and esotericism. His finger-on-lips image expresses the silence and level-headedness required to access mystery and hidden power. In some Hermetic and Alchemical traditions, Harpocrates symbolizes the "Hermetic Mystery" or "Hermetic Arcanum," the knowledge and hidden secrets he guards.

11. So far we have found two definitions about which we can get more information:

    a.   Hermetic Mystery

    b.   Hermetic Arcanum

Here we can use artificial intelligence or our favorite internet browser.

- What is the Hermetic Mystery?

The Hermetic Secret is the knowledge and teaching based on the Hermetic principle and philosophy. Hermetics is an esoteric teaching and philosophical school based on the works of the Egyptian sage **Hermes Trismegistus**.

The Hermetic Mystery encompasses the idea that there is a hidden order in the universe, expressed through principles such as spirit, mentality, and correspondence. It aims to explore and understand the nature of reality and the world..

The Hermetic Mystery also underscores the notion that the All is One and that the mind and consciousness play an important role in the creation and manifestation of reality. It is about the connection between the microcosm (the individual self) and the macrocosm (the universe) and the search for knowledge, wisdom and spiritual insight.

In the Hermetic tradition, the Hermetic secret is considered a valuable and secret knowledge accessible only to the initiated. It incorporates various concepts, practices, and symbols designed to deepen understanding of the universe and promote individual transformation and spiritual development.

- What is the Hermetic Arcanum?

The "Hermetic Arcanum" is a term often used in esoteric and occult traditions. "Arcanum" comes from Latin and means "secret" or "hidden knowledge". The "Hermetic Arcanum" refers to a specific secret or teaching known only to a small group of initiates or chosen ones.

It is believed that this secret contains a deep spiritual, philosophical or magical knowledge that is not intended for the general public. It is seen as something only revealed to those who have reached certain levels of initiation or growth, or have been initiated in certain esoteric traditions.

The "Hermetic Arcanum" can include various things, such as secret rituals, magical practices, mystical teachings or deep philosophical insights. It is often seen as a key to enlightenment, personal transformation, or the unfolding of spiritual potential.

In many esoteric systems and occult traditions, the "Hermetic Arcanum" is viewed as something valuable that should be treated with respect and responsibility. It is often used in the context of secrecy and discretion, to preserve the mystery and sacredness of knowledge and to emphasize the importance of sincere devotion and progress on the spiritual path.

12. The next interesting term in the previous paragraph (11) consists of the phrase: "Hermes Trismegistus".

Who is Hermes Trismegistos?

Hermes Trimegistos is a legendary figure who unites the Greek god Hermes and the Egyptian god Thoth. His name means ' Thrice-greatest' or 'Hermes the Thrice-Wise', reflecting his great wisdom and spirituality. He is the creator of Hermeticism, a philosophy and spirituality based on his writings and teachings.

Hermes Trimegistus is the bearer of divine revelations, the mediator between gods and men, and the teacher of hidden knowledge. His influence was very great in the esoteric tradition and he has had many adherents and interpretations throughout history. It is also associated with knowledge of alchemy, astrology, magic and psychology. Some of his most famous works are the **Emerald Tablet** and the **Kybalion**.

For me, Hermes Trismegistus is an archetype of Lucifer, Satan, or the Devil (we'll see why after a few pages).

13. The author Christian Karl Josias von Bunsen (born Korbach 1791 – Bonn 1860 (+)) mentions in his book: The Place of Egypt in World History (IV) that the god Esmun is known as Sesen, Sôsis, and "The Eighth".

Josias Von Bunsen also mentions that "[This god - Sesen] certainly appears in modern mythology as Thoth (Hermes)".

The idea proposed by Christian Karl Josias von Bunsen that Thoth (Hermes) can be known as Sesen is important for my premise that Hermes Trismegistus (Thoth + Hermes) is a kind of archetype of God's adversary, who in the Christian tradition is called: Lucifer, Satan or simply the devil.

I would like to remark, my Dear Reader, that I, Juan Vitaliano Quiñonez Albán, am Latino (Ecuadorian) and Catholic, so you will not find positive comments about God's adversaries (Lucifer or Satan) in this text.

14. Sesen within different ancestral cultures means several things:

a) In relation to ancient Egyptian culture, it may represent the following:

- A lotus flower.

- A geographic region of ancient Egypt.

 - Another Name of the God Hermes (Thoth).

b) In the antique populace of modern-day Iran, the name Sesen represented an Aramaic deity borne by the Jews during their exile in Babylon. This ancient deity later spread to Europe and centuries later even infiltrated Christianity under the name Saint Sisinnius of Antioch or Saint Sisinnius of Parthia. Regarding the name Sesen, let's first focus on aspects related to Egyptian culture, which are also common in cultures such as the Babylonian and other Canaanite religions due to syncretism.

The lotus flower (sesen) is a solar symbol of creation. According to ancient Egyptian tradition, the lotus flower closes at night and plunges into the water, rising and reopening at dawn. In Hermopolis (city of Hermes in ancient Egypt), the sun god who arose from the chaos of Nun (primeval ocean) emerged as Amen Ra from the petals of a lotus flower. Author Matthew Delooze (2007) identifies this analogy with Freemasonry's "Order out of Chaos" (Ordo ab Chao).

I want to emphasize that for God's Adversary there is what is called syncretism or a merging of cultural or religious ideas. The adversary of God does not want to be unique, but wants to be at least a little present in every religion. For this reason, in this book we will see how we passed from Egyptian culture to Babylonian culture as if they were the same. The customs themselves differ between cultures, but the central philosophy or basis of their so-called belief is the same. Later in the book we will see a detail of this from my point of view.

According to Christian K.J. Bunsen, the ancient city of Hermopolis was called Sesen, Sôsis. This word (Sesen) was derived from an old form of the number six (Ses, SUS).

Author Ralph Ellis associates the word "sesen" with "open" or "breathe". This author even mentions that a possible origin of the word sesame (from the phrase: "Open sesame!") is related to Sesen and its hieroglyph:

sesen (open or breath in English)

Note: There are other hieroglyphs that can also be read as sesen and have a different meaning than the ones I have already explained.

The 1876 book "Half-yearly Compendium of Medical Science" (17-18) published by the University of Michigan identified the hyacinth plant with the word "sesen". This post introduced us to other terms and stated that sesen means also a shoshan in Hebrew and susan in Arabic. However, this identification would be related to the Nymphæa lotus rather than the hyacinth plant.

From now on we will focus on the relationship between Lotus, Shoshan (Lotus in Hebrew) and Susan (Lotus in Arabic).

According to Strong's Hebrew Dictionary, the word 7799 (shushan, shoshan, shoshannah) is a masculine noun and is written as follows: שׁוּשַׁן. If we enter this word into a gematria calculator, we find that it has the numbering 656.

The book Isles of Wonder: the cover story (written by Mason Bigelow) gives us some interesting information about the word shoshan. Where Shoshan, a lily, is identified by some scholars with a lotus flower or an Asiatic buttercup.

In Arabic it is known as Sausan and in Vulgar Arabic as Susan (this has already been mentioned).

Shoshana can represent more than one lily, lotus flower or rose (like Shoshana Jacob). The Midrash mentions the expression "shoshanah shel wered". And the lily rose is one of the symbols of Israel.

Until here I want you to be clear that the lotus, lily, rose and in general any flower can be called shoshan (Hebrew word with a 656 gematria).

2. The Ishtar Gate

(The Eight Gate)

Ištar Gate details. - Babylon, 575 BC (a) A series of lotus-shaped sacral trees with ringed trunks and three terminal corollas connected by stem buds, symbolizing the symbolic theme of eternal return. An example of immortal life (Right Perspective Images/Alamy Stock Photo). (b) The joined trees are framed on four sides by variations of bud and lotus flower motifs (MuseoPics-Paul Williams/Alamy Stock Photo).

Throughout history lilies have been associated with various deities.

The occult author Edain McCoy (2012) tells us that the lily is a Christian symbol of death, while for the goddess Ostara (aka Ēostre) the lily was a symbol used to decorate altars and temples.

Marcia Reiss (2013), on the other hand, is an author who associates the goddess Ostara with a pagan predecessor of the Virgin Mary and equates the lily with a symbol of resurrection in Christianity.

As for Reiss' opinion, I am inclined to agree with Edain McCoy as it would not be the most appropriate to associate the lily with the Virgin Mary since it is a solar symbol (night dies, day is reborn).

From the point of view of fertility, Reiss also associates the Babylonian goddess Ishtar with the lily; and refers to Jacob Grimm, who in his work "Teutonic Mythology" associates the goddess Ishtar with the word "Ostern" (Easter in English) (Easter may be related to Passover or with the East) (the sun rises in the East and dies in the West).

The Babylonian goddess Ishtar was known as Inanna in Sumerian mythology.

Another name by which the Sumerian goddess Inanna was known was Ninsianna.

Ninsianna was also called the Red Queen of Heaven and was considered the personification of the planet Venus.

The planet Venus was named after the goddess with the same name. Goddess of love, fertility and beauty (among other attributes).

The planet Venus is also known by the following names:

- Eosphoros, Greek, means light bearer, and this description was already mentioned in Homer's Iliad.

- Vespers, name mentioned by Virgil and Vesperugo (this name mentioned by Plautus). These names refer to Venus as the evening star.

- Lucifer, Latin, light bearer. One of the names of the morning star in the 1st century BC. according to Cicero.

- Aphrodite, name of the late Greek period.

- Freya, Norse goddess.

Until here we have the following central idea:

Hermes (Thot) (Egyptian deity) is associated with Ishtar, Inanna,

Ninsianna, Venus (Lucifer) through syncretism.

We figured this all out from a translation error (that's why I called this

method **Irrtumlogie**).

שׁוּשׁם = Psst!

(Silence interjection used in Germany)

If we had instead selected the "Detect language" option and then, "Yidis"

was identified, the following wrong translation would have been obtained:

Instead of Psst! We would have gotten the word "Shushas".

Word that happens to be another name of the city of Susa:

Elam	(Gen. 10:22)	Elamites, Elymeans [Susa or Shushas was their capital] with Medes-Madai-Persian Empire.

The city of Susa or Shushan is written in Hebrew as the word lily (lotus or rose) (shushan).

שׁוּשָׁן

Coincidentally Shush! (a word in English similar to Shushas) is used to silence someone:

Shush! is similar to Psst! (used in Germany)

Sshh! would be the equivalent to Psst! in English

The gesture of silence, whether by the goddess Tacita Muta or by Harpocrates (the young Horus), would be a representation of the "Psst!" or the Shush! (in English).

31

THE CREED OF THE SUN AND THE SNAKE

We (Christians or Catholics) who reads this book must be aware that all these apparently coincidences are nothing more than certain characteristics that correspond to an ancient philosophy of Lucifer worship (perhaps not under the term " Lucifer Worship", or through the term "Satan worship"), but rather corresponding to the veneration of two ancestral symbols associated with these archetypes.

And these symbols are: the sun and the snake.

In order to summarize this type of teaching (Philosophy or Belief) without praising it, I will try to be as brief and concise as possible.

1. The forbidden archaeology (understood as the archeology not accepted by the scientific community) tells us that there was a connection between different civilizations worldwide.

Themes such as accounts of a flood as described in the biblical book of Genesis, the idea of a wise man teaching his knowledge and promising to return and the existence of pyramids with common features are specific ideas that support this theory.

2. Regardless of your belief (or disbelief), as the author of this book, I want to make it clear that I respect your point of view.

3. Beyond what forbidden archeology tells us, I want you (Dear Readers) to consider the following criterion; and you will see that what I experienced through gematria is a self-discovery.

A self-discovery that has led me to fight uncomfortable battles with evil, but in a good way has allowed me to strengthen my faith in Jesus.

THE PHILOSOPHY OF THE SUN AND THE SNAKE

I. The philosophy of the sun and the serpent precedes all human civilizations.

II. In order to be able to transfer the philosophy of the sun and the serpent through different peoples, they used titans or legendary sages who, after passing on their knowledge left the land (usually by sea). As they left for their place of origin, these characters promised that they would return.

III. These messengers of the sun and serpent philosophies may have come from an older civilization that was apparently destroyed because its cruelty outweighed its sense of morality.

IV. Among the common traits we find in the civilizations that have adopted this philosophy there are these characteristics:

Architectural Similarities

1. **The Pyramids**: These are structures of sun worship. The Sun is another planet along with Venus with which we can associate God's adversary.

2. **An Eye:** This can be the Eye of Ra or the Eye of Horus and represents the creation that emerged from Chaos. It may represent the pineal gland, which is credited that activates the third eye. It also stands for the idea of the"the god within us".

3. **The misnamed "Flower of Life":** This is a geometric representation derived from the evolution of the third eye, either the Eye of Ra or the Eye of Horus.

4. **Phallic allusions or allusions to the uterus:** These allusions represent symbols of masculinity or femininity.

5. Allusions to the numbers 3, 6, 9 (their multiples and divisors) and geometric figures related to these numbers.

   - Equilateral triangle (pyramid)
   - Hexad (like the Magen David)
   - The Cube (specifically the Cube of Metatron which derives from the Eyes of Ra or Horus).

<u>Symbolic references</u>

1. The reference to the 4 elements: air, water, earth and fire.

2. The Venus Pentacle.

3. The Symbol of the Sun Invictus.

4. The Caduceus.

5. The Rod of Asclepius

Worship of the planets and stars

Another feature of this Sun-Serpent philosophy is the worship or reverence they show not only to the Sun but to other heavenly bodies as well.

After the Sun, Venus is their planet that they worship and adore the most.

Saturn, the planet associated with Satan, is another planet they have among their leaders (planets to worship).

Mars, Jupiter (this one especially in writing), the planet Earth (which they call Mother Earth).

The Sirius star is also considered an object of worship by the followers of this philosophy.

<u>Worship or syncretism towards Jupiter (through texts and books)</u>

Followers of this philosophy used to call God: Iouae.

Iouae was later changed to Jovae. This name sounds kind of similar to the name Jehovah.

Jovae was renamed Jove by the adherents of this philosophy.

Jove is another name for Jupiter or Zeus.

The true name of God is a mystery to all followers of Christ and the God of Israel.

However, by using web applications like "Text to Speech App" I was able to hear a possible name of God. And that name is YEHÓH.

If you doubt about what I'm saying, you can copy and paste the Tetragrammaton יהוה in a "Text to Speech App" and most of the times you will hear the name YEHÓH, but, some Apps will pronounce the Tetragrammaton as Jehovah.

Yeho- is a prefix used in many theophoric names. At this time (2023) there are few texts in which YEHÓH is mentioned as the name of God. However, these texts exist. They're rare, but they exist.

In the Spanish language, God is referred to as "Dios".

This word "God" comes from an Indo-European root: *dyeu-

(The asterisk * used in Indo-European roots indicate that these words are reconstruction of a possible word)

*dyeu- = means: shine, heaven, god, Father Sky, light.

*dyeu- is also an analogy to Lucifer (as a bright star, sun and Jupiter).

I am trying to say that the followers of the Sun-Serpent philosophy, through their scholars and academics, have always attempted to include a reference to God's adversary in the scriptures in which the name of God the Father is mentioned.

Biblia sacra ex Sebastiani Castellionis interpretatione eiusque postrema recognitione parecipue in ususm studiosae juventutis denuo evulgata
(1750)

<u>Leave room for nature – Leave room for nature</u>

This philosophy of the sun and the serpent should not be confused with a religion.

This idea or belief is present in various religions, sects, in magic or even in those people who follow the path of "the god within us".

Nature is beautiful and haunting.

Nature is a creation of God the Father.

Everything moves in nature with a precision that even the best machines today cannot reach.

However in their rituals the followers of this philosophy attempt to control the rain and clouds, and some others will claim to control even natural disasters.

There are rumors of governments manipulating earthquakes through equipment.

They are not interested in controlling nature only through spells and rituals.

If they can find gadgets to mimic a natural disaster, they have no problem with that.

The leaders of the sects who believe in this philosophy are perfect.

Normal people are garbage (according to them).

For the leaders of the cults who believe in this philosophy, we ordinary people are rubbish.

A clear example of this is that, as we all know, they have financed wars, coups (Coups d'etat) and other problems more related to microbiological phenomena.

No les basta con tener dinero de forma obscena.

But they also strive to reduce world population.

Maybe it's not just our poverty that bothers them.

They may also hate the fact that we don't understand the traditions of their ancestors (which are our ancestors too, but most of us did not keep any wealth like them).

Definitely, for whatever reason. The hate they have for us (normal people) is obvious.

Many innocent people have died for this hate.

Meanwhile, they continue to gather themselves in various sects and give them different names. Infiltrating different religions, although basically everything is the same:

1. Sun worshipping.

2. Snake worshipping.

3. Planets and stars worshipping. – They (these elites) attribute an angel, a spirit, and a demon to the planets and stars.

That is, planets have an angel. Planets have an assigned spirit. Planets have an assigned demon.

Like the sun:

Semeliel is its spirit (also might be Shemesh, which is more known).

Nakiel is the angel of the sun.

Sorat is the demon of the sun.

According to Cornelius Agrippa.

4. They (The followers of the Sun-Serpent Philosophy) worship phallic male symbols and female symbols (related to the womb).

These are archetypes of God's adversary: Satan, Lucifer, Isis, Ishtar, Inanna, Venus, Jupiter, the Sun, and others.

There is something called ego or self.

This idea, which I have explored, implies that a deity can be several things at once. Often these things can seem as completely different. But everything is part of the Unity or Oneness.

In this case, Lucifer, who appears only once in the Bible, represents a deity named Helel Ben Sahar.

But at the same time it (Lucifer) represents Samael (also found as deity called Sasm). Samael is better known as Satan.

Satan was once an angel of God, and then he revealed against the God of Israel.

The many egos of God's adversary can result in him having male or female aspects.

Venus, for example, is female.

Venus is associated with Ishtar, Ninsianna and Astarte.

But Venus is also Lucifer.

Another situation that the ego of God's adversary poses are the constant inner conflicts that it (or he) has. Many of these inner conflicts try to make us (humans) believe that they are different deities or different demons.

But, all of them are one.

Zeus, Prometheus, Cronus. They are all different egos of Satan as manifested in different religions or within the same ancient religion.

In general there is always the scene when a heroic son rebels against his Father and then help mortals.

This is a big difference with Jesus, who was always obedient to his Father, even when Death was near.

Horus, Osiris, Isis, they are all the same.

Horus, Osiris and Isis are the different egos of God's adversary.

Isis the mother, we can merge Isis with other mother goddesses. Even with Venus, Aphrodite, Inanna, etc.

Osiris, the cruel father. He is just like Jupiter, Zeus, Baal, EL and other cruel fathers from their various traditions.

Horus, the son who rebels. The rebellious son, who later tries to help or set others free, often in denial of his father, is common in various philosophies or beliefs.

They are all the same.

All egos of God's Adversary are part of the same One or one Ego.

The adversary of God does not seek to be unique; to have an unique cult or rite.

The adversary of God wants to be in every tradition, philosophy, every single ritual of magic or religion, even if it is just in a small part.

Lucifer, is shown in magic as a being of light and knowledge (wisdom, Sophia)

Lucifer is the same as Satan. Satan appears as a dark archetype and for whom magicians must sometimes set up circles of protection, including in them the name of Yahweh in their rituals.

They are equal (Satan = Lucifer).

The adversary of God strives for omnipresence.

The adversary of God seeks the omnipresence that he does not have. While God (Yahweh, YEHÓH, YAH, etc.) is omnipresent.

CONCLUSION

Beyond this battle between good and evil that takes place not only in the real world but also within ourselves, as an author I want to create an awareness in the reader that the Christian religion, be it Catholic, Protestant or Orthodox, MUST NOT allow the infiltration of the philosophy of the sun and the serpent within their creeds or beliefs.

The acceptance of a Christian faith without symbols is a step that Christians must strive for in the future, and it goes beyond the elimination of statues, paintings, murals, engravings and mosaics. We must remove the essence of evil from our symbols, beliefs and most important from our hearts.

This sun and serpent philosophy is far older than any previously known religion and at some point (this philosophy) caused its adherents (be they humans, titans, supermen, celestial beings, etc.) to be annihilated; and if we want to avoid the same faith, we must adhere to the Holy Scriptures and, moreover, follow the teachings of our Lord Jesus Christ.

I say this as a personal opinion; I hope you have enjoyed reading this book and that everything said here (including the method that I thought you) will open your eyes, mind and soul.

The knowledge of these philosophies does not make one an "awakened reader". Believing in these philosophies from a practical point of view does not make one an "awakened reader". What will change your life is to seek a purification of our Christian faith; to help our neighbor as our Lord Jesus Christ did, and to respect those who think differently. But also, being vigorous and resolute against the enemies of the faith.

The change start within ourselves, but not as this philosophy of "the God within us" (like Kabbalah, Rosicrucianism, Freemasonry, etc. said) (include here lef-hand path and righ-hand path magic and others). The change comprises in having the will and determination to accept the truth I am showing you and following Jesus Christ without hesitation.

I usually identify myself as a fiction writer, and I do this as a sort of shield. But tell me if I'm wrong, because if I'm wrong I would correct my mistake, but if you tell me that "the pentagram of Venus" is a positive symbol, that the flower of life brings changes for the better, or things like that, I would rather warn you (if you were a Christian) that you are misled by the most ancient philosophy of our civilization and that the easiest and better way of finding truth would be following Jesus.

So, here is wisdom. Let the one who hath the inside reckon the number of the beast, for it is a human number (…)

Follow this book method and you will find the wisdom and the insight. At 17 years old I learnt what most 17s Catholic guys know. But now, that I have past my 30s, I have learnt, what I taught you here in this book.

Thank you very much.

PARERGA ET PARALIPOMENA

The following pages of this Supplement are in Spanish

GUIÓN DE VIDEO

Debido a nuestras fuertes convicciones personales, deseamos enfatizar que este video de ninguna manera respalda una creencia en el ocultismo.

I) Para entender el cálculo del número de la bestia, veamos una breve cronología de las traducciones de la Biblia.

La Biblia es una colección de textos religiosos, escritos o escrituras sagradas para las personas religiosas. Aparece en forma de antología, una compilación de textos de una variedad de formas que están todos vinculados por la creencia de que son colectivamente revelaciones de Dios. Estos textos incluyen relatos históricos enfocados teológicamente, himnos, oraciones, proverbios, parábolas, cartas didácticas, admoniciones, ensayos, poesía y profecías. Los creyentes generalmente también consideran que la Biblia es un producto de la inspiración divina.

Los libros que una tradición o grupo incluye en la Biblia se denominan canónicos, lo que indica que la tradición/grupo ve la colección como la verdadera representación de la palabra y la voluntad de Dios. Han evolucionado varios cánones bíblicos, con contenidos superpuestos y divergentes de una denominación a otra. La Biblia hebrea comparte la mayor parte de su contenido con su antigua traducción griega, la Septuaginta, que a su vez fue la base del ANTIGUO TESTAMENTO cristiano. El Nuevo Testamento cristiano es una colección de escritos de los primeros cristianos, que se creía que eran discípulos judíos de Cristo, escritos en griego koiné del primer siglo.

b. El siguiente video está basado en la Vulgata Católica

¿Qué es la Vulgata Católica?

La Vulgata es una traducción latina de la Biblia de finales del siglo IV. Se convertiría en la versión latina de la Biblia promulgada oficialmente por la Iglesia Católica durante el siglo XVI como la Vulgata Sixtina y luego como la Vulgata Clementina; la Vulgata todavía se usa actualmente en la Iglesia latina.

La traducción fue en gran parte obra de Jerónimo de Stridon quien, en 382, había sido comisionado por el Papa Dámaso I para revisar los Evangelios Vetus Latina* utilizados por la Iglesia Romana. Por iniciativa propia, amplió esta labor de revisión y traducción para incluir la mayor parte de los libros de la Biblia. Una vez publicada, la nueva versión fue ampliamente adoptada. Durante los siglos siguientes, finalmente eclipsó a la Vetus Latina.

* = Actualmente no pudimos obtener un pdf de los textos de Vetus Latina (si tiene uno, envíenos un correo electrónico a: ancientsecretswisdom@gmail.com)

c. ¿Qué dice la Vulgata Católica de Apocalipsis 13:18 (donde se menciona el número de la bestia)?

18 hic sapientia est qui habet intellectum conputet numerum bestiae numerus enim hominis est et numerus eius est sescenti sexaginta sex

"Aquí hay sabiduría. El que tiene entendimiento, cuente el número de la bestia. Porque es el número de un hombre: y el número de él es seiscientos sesenta y seis".

Tenga en cuenta que el número infame de la bestia está escrito en palabras (en esta traducción -La Vulgata-)

Sescenti sexaginta sex

d. Entonces tenemos esta situación.

1. El Nuevo Testamento fue escrito en griego koiné del siglo I.

2. Uno de los compendios más conocidos, "La Vulgata", fue escrito en latín en el siglo IV (trescientos años después de los primeros textos escritos en griego koiné).

Entonces, aquí tenemos un problema...

e. Sobre la autoría de la Vulgata Latina

La Vulgata tiene un texto compuesto que no es del todo obra de Jerónimo. La traducción de Jerónimo de los cuatro Evangelios son revisiones de las traducciones de Vetus Latina que hizo teniendo el griego como referencia.

Las traducciones latinas del resto del Nuevo Testamento son revisiones de la Vetus Latina, presuntamente realizadas por círculos pelagianos o por Rufinus el Sirio, o por Rufinus de Aquileia.

Varios libros no revisados del Antiguo Testamento de la Vetus Latina también se incluyeron comúnmente en la Vulgata. Estos son: 1 y 2 Macabeos, Sabiduría, Eclesiástico, Baruc y la Carta de Jeremías.

Habiendo traducido por separado el libro de los Salmos del griego Hexapla Septuagint, Jerome tradujo todos los libros de la Biblia judía, incluido el libro hebreo de los Salmos, del propio hebreo. También tradujo los libros de Tobit y Judith de las versiones arameas, las adiciones al Libro de Ester de la Septuaginta común y las adiciones al Libro de Daniel del griego de Teodoción.

f. ¿Seiscientos sesenta y seis o 616?

Aunque Ireneo (siglo II d. C.) afirmó que el número era 666 y reportó varios errores de escritura del número, los teólogos tienen dudas sobre la lectura tradicional debido a la aparición de la cifra 616 en el Codex Ephraemi Rescriptus (C; París, uno de los cuatro grandes códices unciales), así como en la versión latina de Tyconius (DCXVI, ed. Souter en el Journal of Theology, SE, abril de 1913), y en una versión armenia antigua (ed. Conybeare, 1907). Ireneo conocía la lectura del 616, pero no la adoptó (Haer. V, 30). En la década de 380, al corregir la versión en latín existente del Nuevo Testamento (comúnmente conocida como Vetus Latina), Jerónimo retuvo "666".

g. ¿Cómo se escribe seiscientos sesenta y seis en números romanos?

Si recordamos en este video la Vulgata mencionó una palabra para el número seiscientos sesenta y seis:

Sescenti sexaginta sex

DCLXVI

DC = 600

LX = 60

VI = 6

Este número romano es bastante conocido dentro de las comunidades cristianas y creyentes. Algunas interpretaciones se han hecho sin usar la isopsefia griega, como:

Vicarius Filii Dei

Que es una frase utilizada por primera vez en la donación medieval falsificada de Constantino para referirse a San Pedro, un líder de la Iglesia cristiana primitiva y considerado como el primer Papa por la Iglesia Católica.

```
V =   5
I =   1
C = 100
A =   0        F =   0
R =   0        I =   1
I =   1        L =  50        D = 500
V =   5        I =   1        E =   0
S =   0        I =   1        I =   1
    ─────          ─────          ─────
    112    +       53    +       501    =   666
```

Y como se ve obviamente algunos números equivalen a "cero", por lo que en nuestra opinión, no creemos que esta polémica sea acertada (al menos como se expresa).

h. ¿Y si el número DCLXVI tiene otro significado no conocido hasta ahora?

Pensamos como hipótesis que esto podría ser posible. Entonces, estamos proponiendo a través de este video que el número DCLXVI podría ser un código que debe ser transliterado, lo que significa cambiar los símbolos en letras.

- Basado en la pronunciación indicada por el sitio web: PHONETICA LATINÆ - Cómo pronunciar latín

https://la.raycui.com/alphabet.html

Cambiaremos cada una de las letras de DCLXVI por sus fonemas en latín eclesiástico:

(Si desea escuchar los sonidos (fonemas o vocablos), visite el sitio web referido)

DCLXVI

De che el iks ve i

o

De che-el-iks ve-i

Aparentemente, esta transliteración puede parecer una galimatía pero, reorganizándola:

dē celix vei

Que se traduciría en:

dē (abajo, lejos de)

celix (Cilicia la tierra de celix) = Celliks o Celli significa celtas

vei (de la palabra vai -ir-)

Esto como una hipótesis podría interpretarse como

"Lejos de los Celtas Va"

(Si alguien que ve este video puede debatir esto, cualquier objeción será bien recibida.)

i.) El libro: Hechos de los Apóstoles de Marcos Dávila (2019).

Cilicia (Strong's 2791) significa "la tierra de Celix" que, en inglés simple, significa Lands of Celts.

j. ¿Quiénes eran los celtas?

Los celtas o los Celix (también deletreados con K y Kelliks pronunciados) eran descendientes de tribus celtas del centro de Europa.

h. Cálculo de isopsefia

En copto hay más referencias relativamente difundidas entre los cristianos como:

1) Teitan

The value of the Coptic Letters is:—

T	T	.	.	.	.	.	.	300
ε	E	.	.	.	.	.	.	5
I	I	.	.	.	.	.	.	10
T	T	.	.	.	.	.	.	300
₳	A	.	.	.	.	.	.	1
ⲛ	N	.	.	.	.	.	.	50
								666

Tomado de The Natural Genesis escrito por Gerald Massey en 1883

i. Cálculo del número a través de la Gematria hebrea y del Traductor de Google para personas que no hablan hebreo (Irrtumlogie o Irrtumlogía. – cálculo erróneo nos permite llegar a un dato de carácter esotérico, espiritual, bíblico, filosófico o relacionado a estos)

I) Aquí hay dos formas:

a. Buscar una combinación de números cuya suma (adición) sea igual a 666, como 300+300+60+6 = shim + shim + samej + vav = ש + ש + ס + ו

Y una vez que tenemos las combinaciones de números cambiamos de lugar hasta que el Traductor de Google nos proporcione una "traducción lógica" como por ejemplo:

Shushas

Si desea ver lo que significa SHUSHAS y su relación con el número seiscientos sesenta y seis, consulte nuestro video anterior titulado: Lucifer, Ishtar y el símbolo Lily-Rose. O en la búsqueda de YOUTUBE: "Ishtar and the Number of the Beast" o "Lucifer, Ishtar and the Lily-Rose symbol"

b. Y la otra forma que es un poco más larga (según nuestro criterio) es que:

- Vaya y busque un libro donde aparezca una palabra hebrea (preferiblemente en pdf, sin imagen escaneada).

- Ir al sitio web:

https://www.torahcalc.com/gematria/

- Recomendamos la Mispar Gadol (Large Sofit) Gematria en el mismo sitio web.

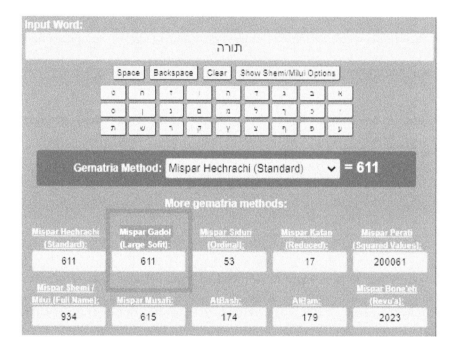

Esto para evitar la simplificación de números (lo que significa que si una palabra tiene una gematría de seiscientos sesenta y seis, podría reducirse a 106 o algo así).

Aquí encontrará en el Libro del Génesis de Gerald Massey (1883) algunas palabras interesantes que son seiscientas sesenta y seis gematría.

ש	(S)	.	.	.	.	.	300
ע	(A)	.	.	.	.	.	70
ר	(R)	.	.	.	.	.	200
ו	(O)	.	.	.	.	.	6
צ	(S)	.	.	.	.	.	90
							666

SAROS (El saros es un período de exactamente 223 meses sinódicos, aproximadamente 6585,3211 días, o 18 años, 10, 11 o 12 días (dependiendo del número de años bisiestos), y 8 horas, que se pueden utilizar para predecir eclipses de Sol y Luna). Un período saros después de un eclipse, el Sol, la Tierra y la Luna vuelven aproximadamente a la misma geometría relativa, una línea casi recta, y ocurrirá un eclipse casi idéntico, en lo que se conoce como un ciclo de eclipse).

Sut or Sevekh was Saturn under his Planetary Type, and in Chaldee Saturn is Satur, *i.e. Stur*, and the numerical value is :

ס	S	.	.	.	.	.	60
ת	T	.	.	.	.	.	400
ו	U	.	.	.	.	.	6
ר	R	.	.	.	.	.	200
							666

Y si recordamos el lirio-rosa (relacionado con Ishtar en videos pasados) encontraremos lo siguiente:

Elliot[1] has observed () that the Kabalists used to ask *"What is the Lily?"* (Shushnah) in the Book of Esther, rendered by Shushan as a proper name in the A.V., *"because both words contained the same numerical value."* This is given as the No. 661.

ש	300	א	1
ו	6	ס	60
ש	300	ת	400
ן	50	ר	200
ה	5		
	——		——
	661		661
	——		——

But this is to miss the secret meaning. It may be supposed that the Kabalists would use the *He* for "*the* Lily," and also write the name *Hesther* in accordance with

that of *Hadash*. The He adds five, making the number 666. Hesther is the Hebrew form of Ishtar or Shetar (Eg.) the Betrothed, and the character of the Betrothed is performed by Hesther for twelve months.[1] The Kabbalistic conceit of "the Lily," Hesther, and the mystical number is precisely the same as that of the Beast.

The Lotus-Lily was a symbol of the genitrix or Virgin-Mother, who sat upon the Waters as the Scarlet Lady of mystery and abomination. The Sistrum was another symbol of the Beast Hes. Isis, or "Seses," a Gnostic name of Isis. Its name of *Seshesh* contains the three S's, value 666. These were represented by the three wires, that make it a figure or image of the number 666.

Astarte, also, in a dual or compound character called Isis-Minerva, has been found under the title of Saosis or 666 when the S's are read according to the numerical value of the letters. The Beast was of both sexes, according to the double Constellation of the Seven Stars.

Eso es todo lo que tenemos que decir sobre este asunto, al menos por ahora.

Dear Reader

If you have reached this instance of the book

Thank you Very Much

Juan Vitaliano Quinonez Alban

(J.V.Q.A)

ABOUT THE AUTHOR

Juan Vitaliano Quiñonez Albán is an Ecuadorian writer of themes such as fantasy, religion, mythology and artificial intelligence.

He has published several books in Spanish and English containing both fictional and non-fictional elements. His works are inspired by various sources such as the Bible, apocryphal literature, ancient history, esotericism, numerology and gematria.

His most famous books include:

El Anticristo y la Inteligencia Artificial (The Antichrist and the Artificial Intelligence), a series of two volumes that tells a fictional story about the end of times, based on a dialogue he has with an artificial intelligence through an online chat application had.

Sabiduría de los Antiguos Secretos (Wisdom of the Ancient Secrets), a book that provides an introduction to the study of the ancient mysteries, which he calls Ancient Secrets Wisdom, or The Secret Teachings. He explains some concepts like gematria, numerology, symbolism and mythology from his Christian perspective.

The Logos - The Word of Jesus Christ [ὁ Λόγος], a compilation of quotations from Jesus Christ according to the Gospel of St. Matthew. He analyzes each quotation in the context of its meaning and its relationship to other biblical passages.

His books are available on various online platforms and applications.

Ingram Content Group UK Ltd.
Milton Keynes UK
UKHW020731060623
422954UK00015B/827